Paddington
and the
Marmalade
Maze

First published in hardback in Great Britain by HarperCollins Publishers Ltd in 1987
First published in paperback by Collins Picture Lions in 2001
New edition published by HarperCollins Children's Books in 2009
This edition published in 2014

7 9 10 8 6

ISBN: 978-0-00-710768-1

Collins Picture Lions is an imprint of HarperCollins Publishers Ltd.
HarperCollins Children's Books is a division of HarperCollins Publishers Ltd.

Text copyright © Michael Bond 1987
Illustrations copyright © R. W. Alley 1999

Visit our website at: www.harpercollins.co.uk

Printed in China

Michael Bond
Paddington
and the
Marmalade
Maze

Illustrated by R. W. Alley

HarperCollins *Children's Books*

One day, Paddington's friend, Mr Gruber, took him on an outing to a place called Hampton Court Palace.

"I think you will enjoy it, Mr Brown," he said as they drew near. "It's very old and it has over one thousand rooms. Lots of Kings and Queens have lived here."

Paddington always enjoyed his outings with Mr Gruber and he couldn't wait to see inside the Palace.

As they made their way through an arch, Mr Gruber pointed to a large clock.

"That's a very special clock," he said. "It not only shows the time, it tells you what month it is."

"Perhaps we should hurry, Mr Gruber," said Paddington anxiously. "It's half past June already."

They hadn't been inside the Palace very long before they came across a room which had the biggest bed Paddington had ever seen.

"Queen Anne used to sleep in it," said Mr Gruber.

"I expect they put the rope round it to stop her falling out when she had visitors," said Paddington, looking at all the people.

"This is known as the 'Haunted Gallery',"
said Mr Gruber. "They do say that when
Catherine Howard's ghost passes by you
can feel a cold draught."

Paddington shivered. "I hope she's got
a duffle coat like mine!" he said.

Mr Gruber took Paddington to see the
kitchen next.

"In the old days they used wood fires,"
he explained. "That's why there
is such a high ceiling. There
was a lot of smoke."

"I was hoping they might have left some
Royal buns behind," said Paddington, licking
his lips.

"Talking of buns," said Mr Gruber, "I think it's time we had our lunch."

He led the way outside and they sat down together on the edge of a pool.

As Paddington opened his suitcase he accidentally dropped one of his sandwiches into the water. It was soon alive with goldfish.

"They must like marmalade," said Mr Gruber. "I wonder if that's how they got their name?"

When they had finished their sandwiches,
Mr Gruber took Paddington to see 'The
Great Vine'.

"It's very famous," he said. "Every year
they pick over five hundred bunches
of grapes. Imagine that,
Mr Brown!"

"I'm trying to, Mr Gruber," said Paddington.
"I think I might plant a grape pip when I get
back home."

Mr Gruber chuckled. "I'm afraid you
will have a long wait, Mr Brown," he said.
"That vine is over two hundred
years old."

"Now," said Mr Gruber, "before we leave we must visit the famous maze. Sometimes it takes people hours to find their way out."

"I hope that doesn't happen to us," said Paddington. "My paws are getting tired."

"Perhaps it's time I took you home," said Mr Gruber.

Much to his surprise, the words were no sooner out of his mouth than everyone around them began to talk.

"Hey, that sounds a great idea," said a man in a striped shirt.

"Please to wait while I buy a new film for my camera," said a Japanese lady.

"I've never been inside a real English home before," said another lady. "I wonder if they serve tea?

"Oh, dear!" whispered Mr Gruber. "They must think I'm one of the guides. What shall we do?"

"Mrs Bird won't be very pleased if they all follow us home," exclaimed Paddington. "She only has a small teapot."

Then he had an idea.

"Follow me," he called. "I think perhaps we ought to go in the maze after all."

"Are you sure we are doing the right thing?" gasped Mr Gruber, as he hurried on behind.

"Bears are good at mazes," said Paddington. "You need to be in Darkest Peru. The forests are very thick."

And sure enough, before Mr Gruber had time to say any more, Paddington led the way out, leaving everyone else inside.

"How ever did you manage to do that, Mr Brown?" gasped Mr Gruber.

"Quickest visit I've ever seen," agreed the man in the ticket office.

"I used marmalade chunks to show where we had been," said Paddington. "It's something my Aunt Lucy taught me before she went into the Home For Retired Bears."

"But I thought you had eaten all your sandwiches," said Mr Gruber.

"I always keep a spare one under my hat in case I have an emergency," said Paddington. "That's something else Aunt Lucy taught me. She'll be very pleased when she hears."

And he stopped at a kiosk to buy a picture postcard so that he could write and tell her all about his day out.

That night when he went to bed, as well as the postcard and a pen, Paddington took some rope.

"It's something Queen Anne used to do," he announced. "I've a lot to tell Aunt Lucy and I don't want to fall out of bed before I've finished."

Collect all the fantastic books about Paddington!

FICTION

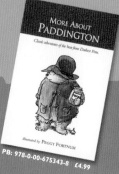

A BEAR CALLED PADDINGTON
PB: 978-0-00-717416-4 £4.99
HB: 978-0-00-714187-6 £9.99

A BEAR CALLED PADDINGTON
CD Audio: £9.99
978-0-00-716165-2

MORE ABOUT PADDINGTON
CD Audio: £9.99
978-0-00-716168-3

MORE ABOUT PADDINGTON
PB: 978-0-00-675343-8 £4.99

PADDINGTON MARCHES ON
PB: 978-0-00-675362-9 £4.99

PADDINGTON TAKES THE TEST
PB: 978-0-00-675378-0 £4.99

PADDINGTON HELPS OUT
PB: 978-0-00-675344-5 £4.99

PADDINGTON ABROAD
PB: 978-0-00-675345-2 £4.99

PADDINGTON AT LARGE
PB: 978-0-00-675363-6 £4.99

PADDINGTON AT WORK
PB: 978-0-00-675367-4 £4.99

PADDINGTON ON TOP!
PB: 978-0-00-675377-3 £4.99

PADDINGTON TAKES THE AIR
PB: 978-0-00-675379-7 £4.99

PADDINGTON GOES TO TOWN
PB: 978-0-00-675366-7 £4.99

PADDINGTON HERE AND NOW
HB: 978-0-00-726940-2 £10.99
PB: 978-0-00-726941-9 £4.99
Audio CD:
978-0-00-727086-6 £11.99

PICTURE BOOKS

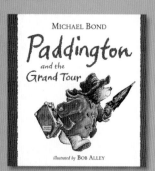

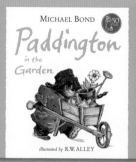

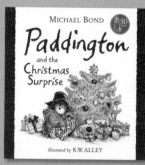

Paddington and the Grand Tour
PB: 978-0-00-712314-8 £5.99
PB & Audio CD: 978-0-00-728234-0 £7.99

Paddington
HB: 978-0-00-723632-9 £10.99
PB: 978-0-00-723633-6 £5.99
PB & Audio CD: 978-0-00-725655-6 £7.99

Paddington in the Garden
PB: 978-0-00-712316-2 £5.99
PB & Audio CD: 978-0-00-728233-3 £7.99

Paddington and the Christmas Surprise
PB: 978-0-00-725773-7 £5.99
PB & Audio CD: 978-0-00-728236-4 £7.99

ALSO AVAILABLE

Paddington at the Carnival • PB: 978-0-00-664725-6 • £5.99
Paddington at the Zoo • PB: 978-0-00-664744-7 • £5.99
Paddington at the Palace • PB: 978-0-00-710440-6 • £5.99
Paddington's Suitcase • 978-0-00-725194-0 • £14.99
Paddington My Book of Marmalade • HB: 978-0-00-726946-6 • £5.99
A Bear Called Paddington – 50th Anniversary edition • HB: 978-0-00-726196-3 • £14.99